The Berenstain Bears
BLAZE A TRAIL

Through deepest wood
and darkest trail –
Will the Bear Scout march
succeed or fail?

A TRAIL

Stan & Jan Berenstain

Random House 🏠 New York

Copyright © 1987 by Berenstains, Inc. All rights reserved under International and Pan-American Copyright Conventions. Published in the United States by Random House, Inc., New York, and simultaneously in Canada by Random House of Canada Limited, Toronto.

Library of Congress Cataloging-in-Publication Data: Berenstain, Stan. The Berenstain bears blaze a trail. (A first time reader) SUMMARY: Bumbling Papa Bear tries to help the Bear Scouts earn their merit badges in hiking. [1. Hiking—Fiction. 2. Bears—Fiction. 3. Stories in rhyme] I. Berenstain, Jan. II. Title. III. Series: Berenstain, Stan. First time reader. PZ8.3.B4493BgT 1987 [E] 87-4552 ISBN: 0-394-89132-5 (trade); 0-394-99132-X (lib. bdg.)

Manufactured in the United States of America   27 28 29 30

"This way, Scouts!"
Brother Bear said.
"Let's go while Papa
is still in bed!
Let's blaze a trail
through the wood,
by ourselves,
the way Scouts should!"

But Papa was *not*
still in bed.
He was waiting for them
up ahead....
"This way, Scouts!
Let's blaze that trail!
With me along
you cannot fail!"

"Wait," said Brother,
"for Scout Leader Jane.
Look! Here she comes now
in her plane.
She's going to watch us
from the air!"
She wasn't too pleased
to see Papa Bear.

"What you Scouts need
is a guide like me!
I'll get you those badges!
Come! You'll see!

"This way, Scouts! That way is wrong. That twisty way will take too long!"

"But, Papa! The guidebook says:
'When blazing a trail
through swamp or bog,
NEVER step on a sunken log!...'"

"And that log," said Sister,
"is a crocodile!"
Pa blazed that trail
Papa Bear style!

"Wow!" said Fred.
"This is good!
A whole new trail
right through the wood!"

"That," bragged Papa,
"is a good lesson for you.
Just get up speed
and crash right through!"

" 'Now, mark the trail,' "
Sister read from the book,
" 'so others can follow
the path you took.' "

"Pooh!" said Papa.
"Twig signs are not for me.
 Here! Watch this—
 I use a tree!"

Then he went flying
through the air—
into a nest! An eagle's nest!

"Just thought I'd drop in," said Papa Bear.

The Scouts marched on
through the wood,
but soon the trail
was not so good.

"This won't last,"
said Papa Bear.
"While I was up that tree
back there,
I could see
for miles around.
Come! This is the way
to higher ground!"

"This ground is good.
It's higher and drier.
Just the place
for our cooking fire."

"But, Pop," said Brother.
"We don't need to cook.
We have our trail rations.
Lots of them! Look!"

"Trail rations? Pooh!
I'll cook up a batch
of my delicious
trailblazer stew!"

"When on the trail,
wild things are best!
All cooked up
in an old bird's nest!

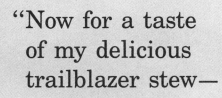

"Now for a taste
of my delicious
trailblazer stew—

...PEW!"

"On second thought,
stew's not on my diet.
Er—about that trail food—
I think I'll try it!

"Come!" shouted Papa.
"Your merit badges
are almost won!
Through Rocky Gorge,
and the test is done!"

"Shush, Papa! Shush!
It says in the guide:
'In rocky places do not shout—
a noise can cause rocks to slide!'"

But Sister's warning
came too late.
"Can't hear!" shouted Pa.
"The noise of these rocks
is much too great!"

Then Jane, who was watching
all the while,
landed her plane
on Pa's rock pile.

"Your merit badges!"
the scout leader said.
"For Brother...for Sister...
for Cousin Fred!
And one badge more..."
added Leader Jane.
"One for Papa!
I shall explain."

"Papa, you blazed a trail.
You did it fast.
Your three landmarks
are sure to last.

"First, we have Crocodile Alley,
thanks to you—

"Second, the smell
made by your stew.

"The third landmark
I have in mind
is the great rock pile
you left behind!"

"We did it, Scouts!
We knew we could.
We did what
we said we would.
We won badges
to wear with pride
by following
our Bear Scout Guide!"

4